The Legend of the Lonesome Bear

Contents

Written by Juliette Mack
Illustrated by Anton Petrov

The Camping Trip

Ricky poked his nose out from under the blankets. It was still before six in the morning, much too early to get up, and it was freezing cold. Even in his room there was no mistaking the chill. Winter was definitely on its way.

Even though it was cold, Ricky was too excited to stay in bed for long! Today they would leave for their camping trip. Every year, Ricky's dad took him and his sister Dee camping. This year was extra special, because Grandpa was coming as well.

Ricky couldn't wait to show Grandpa the best fishing spot, and where to put the food so that the animals couldn't get it, and – oh, there was so much to tell him!

Ricky looked at the clock – nearly six. It was still too early, but if he was quiet he wouldn't wake anyone.

Quietly, Ricky got dressed. His backpack was sitting in the corner. He had packed it three days ago, and finally the big day was here! Ricky went down to the kitchen.

"Hello," said his dad. He was making breakfast. "Couldn't you sleep?"

"Dad!" yelled Ricky. "What are you doing up so early?"

"Getting things ready for the camping trip, and cooking breakfast," his dad replied.

Grandpa walked in smiling and holding Dee's hand. "Do you need another helper?" he asked.

"Grandpa!" squealed Ricky. "When did you get here?"

"Shhhh! Keep the noise down. Your mother's still asleep," Dad said.

"Sorry," whispered Ricky. "So, when did you arrive?" he asked Grandpa again.

"I got here late last night, when you and Dee were already asleep," said Grandpa. "Now, let's eat breakfast and pack the car."

Before long, they had eaten, the car was packed, and they were ready to go.

Ricky's mother came into the kitchen sleepily.

"Have a good trip," she said, as they all got into the car with their dog, Rex. "See you soon. Be careful."

When they arrived at the camp seven hours later, Grandpa said, "I'm glad we're here. That was a long trip."

Ricky and Dee ran all around the camp. Everything was just as they remembered it from last year. Rex barked happily after them.

"Can we go fishing now, Dad?" asked Ricky.

"You know the rules, Ricky," answered Dad. "We always get the camp sorted out and the tents set up before anything else."

They all worked hard for the next few hours setting up the camp and gathering firewood. Everything was ready just as it was getting dark. Ricky's dad lit the fire and cooked dinner.

"Enjoy your meal," he said as he put the plates down. "This could be our last big meal for a while if we don't catch any fish tomorrow!"

"Dad!" groaned Ricky and Dee together. "You say that every year and we always catch a lot of fish!"

They were sitting around the fire, toasting marshmallows, when suddenly they heard an eerie sound. It was a cross between a roar, a grunt, and a growl!

"What was that?" shivered Ricky. He pulled his sleeping bag close around him and moved closer to the fire.

"Ah," said Grandpa, "that sounds to me like the Lonesome Bear."

"Do you mean a grizzly bear?" asked Dee, moving closer to Grandpa.

"No, I don't mean a grizzly bear," said Grandpa, "I mean the Lonesome Polar Bear."

"Grandpa," said Ricky, "we know that polar bears live in the ice and snow in the Arctic, not here in Canada."

"But this is no ordinary bear," said Grandpa. "Haven't I told you the legend of the Lonesome Bear?"

"No, Grandpa, tell us!" Ricky and Dee said together.

Grandpa smiled and moved his chair closer to the fire.

"I was about your age when my grandfather told me the story," he said. "He heard it from his grandfather, who probably heard the story from his grandfather, so I guess it's about time I told you."

Grandpa put a marshmallow on a stick into the fire, and began the story.

The Legend of the Lonesome Bear

Many years ago, long before you or I were born, the Inuit people lived in the Arctic in harmony with all the Arctic creatures, big and small. There were caribou with their big antlers, birds, seals, whales, and, of course, the mighty polar bears.

The Inuit people hunted animals for food and to make clothing and blankets out of their skin and fur. They never hunted too much, though. They only killed to take care of their needs. And they always used every part of an animal.

One year, a polar bear was born who was different from other polar bears. Although he romped and played in the den with his brother and sister, he preferred sleeping.

"Come on, lazy bones," the other cubs said to him. "Come and hunt with us."

But the little polar bear would smile lazily, roll over, and go back to sleep. While his brother and sister grew big and strong and hunted for food, he slept. While they learned how to swim and hide from hunters, he slept.

When they were a year old, the polar-bear cubs were big enough and strong enough to go out on their own. Their mother had watched them play, and she knew that they would be able to hunt for food and hide from hunters.

The lazy polar bear, however, knew nothing. He had been too busy sleeping to learn how to survive on his own.

The polar-bear cubs set out from the den one fine frosty morning. They walked for a while, but soon the lazy bear was tired and had to stop.

"Don't leave me!" he cried out to his brother and sister. "Wait for me!"

They didn't wait. They just kept going.

"You should have spent more time awake, growing healthy and strong, and less time sleeping," they called back to him. "Maybe then you would be able to keep up with us!"

And with that, they marched off, leaving him sitting on the ice. All alone, the little bear trudged back to the den.

"I'll just stay home with my mother," he thought.

But his mother had other ideas.

"You should have listened to me more when you were growing up," she said. "You shouldn't have spent so much time being lazy, and then you'd be able to survive in the Arctic on your own."

The lazy little polar bear looked very sad as his mother jumped into the water and swam away.

"If only I had learned how to swim," he thought. "Then I could have gone with my mother!"

The lazy polar bear was alone, and now he was hungry. He didn't know how to hunt, so he couldn't catch any caribou. He didn't know how to swim, so he couldn't catch any seals. He started to walk.

The little bear walked and walked for miles and miles, until he was lost. He was tired and hungry and didn't know what to do, so he lay down on the ice and cried himself to sleep.

The Inuit Village

The next morning, the sound of voices woke the little bear up.

"I must be near a village," he said to himself. "I bet they'll have some food for me."

Quietly he crept up to the village. There were people everywhere. His white fur blended well with the snow, so the people didn't notice him. He spied some meat hanging up. His mouth watered. He was so hungry that he almost ran right into the village to grab the meat.

"No," he told himself, "I'll wait until night to get the meat. It'll be safer then."

So the little polar bear went off into the snow to wait for night. When darkness fell, he crept back to the village again. It was quiet. Everyone was asleep. He crept along to where the meat was hanging. He pulled it down and ran off into the night with it.

It was so good! He ate and he ate until all the meat was gone and then he fell into a deep sleep.

The next day, the whole village was in an uproar over the stolen meat.

"Someone or something has been here!" the people said to each other. "We must hang the meat higher off the ground."

That day, while the little bear slept, the hunters went to catch more food for their families to eat.

As night fell, the little bear woke up.

"What a good idea that was!" he said to himself. "I don't have to know how to hunt for food. I can just take it from this village. How stupid my brother and sister were to waste time learning how to hunt and swim when they could just take food from villages. I don't need my brother and sister. I'm doing just fine all on my own."

When it was really dark, the polar bear crept back into the village. The hunters had killed a caribou. The meat was hanging a little higher, but the polar bear stretched up and pulled it down. He ran off into the night with his food. "This is so easy!" he thought as he ran off.

In the morning, the villagers woke to find that once again their meat had been stolen. The hunters went off to hunt again, while the elders planned how to catch the thief.

That night, a guard watched the meat to see who or what was taking it. Once again, the polar bear came for his meal. The hunters were furious.

"We'll track that bear and shoot him!" they yelled.

But the elders of the village were wise.

"No," they said. "We must teach this bear that it is not his place to get food from us. Bears should get their food in the wild. We will talk to the wise man. He will know what to do."

Caught in the Act!

The elders sent a young boy to the next village to fetch the wise man.

The wise man told the elders his idea. That night, the villagers waited with a net. When the bear came for his meal, they caught him in the net!

Then, the wise man went up close to the little bear and blew some stardust into his face. Now the bear would be able to understand what he was saying.

"You have chosen to live away from your family," said the wise man to the little bear. "You did not learn how to hunt or swim. You did not learn the ways of the polar bear. From now on, you must wander the earth all alone. You will not be seen by people ever again."

"And," the wise man said sternly, "you will repay these people for the meat you took from them. You will stop any other bears from stealing people's food. You will act as a warning signal for every human on earth, forever. If a bear is approaching people, you must warn them by growling as loudly as you can. This is your punishment."

And with that, the wise man lifted the net, and the little polar bear ran away into the snow and vanished without a trace.

Things That Go Bump in the Night

"They say," Grandpa finished, "that the lonesome polar bear always growls and bellows to warn people when grizzly bears are approaching."

Ricky and Dee looked at each other and shivered.

"Are you saying that the noise we heard before was the Lonesome Polar Bear?" asked Dee doubtfully.

"Who knows?" said Grandpa. "I've never heard that growling before. It could be."

"Does that mean there's a bear coming for us right now?" asked Dee, looking frightened.

Just then, they heard a sound in the bushes!

Ricky screamed.

"It's the bear!" yelled Dee.

"Woof, woof! Woof, woof!" And Rex bounded out from the trees, and ran up to them.

"Rex!" Ricky shouted. "You scared us!"

"There isn't really a lonesome bear out there, is there?" asked Ricky. "You just made that story up to frighten us, didn't you, Grandpa?"

Grandpa just raised his eyebrows.

"Ignore the legend at your own risk, Ricky," he said. "I'm going to check that our food is hung up high before I go to bed!"